Big Bad Beans

Beverly Lewis

Beverly Lewis Books for Young Readers

PICTURE BOOKS

Annika's Secret Wish
Cows in the House
Just Like Mama

THE CUL-DE-SAC KIDS

The Double Dabble Surprise
The Chicken Pox Panic
The Crazy Christmas Angel Mystery
No Grown-ups Allowed
Frog Power
The Mystery of Case D. Luc
The Stinky Sneakers Mystery
Pickle Pizza
Mailbox Mania
The Mudhole Mystery
Fiddlesticks
The Crabby Cat Caper
Tarantula Toes
Green Gravy
Backyard Bandit Mystery
Tree House Trouble
The Creepy Sleep-Over
The Great TV Turn-Off
Piggy Party
The Granny Game
Mystery Mutt
Big Bad Beans
The Upside-Down Day
The Midnight Mystery

Katie and Jake and the Haircut Mistake

www.BeverlyLewis.com

THE CUL-DE-SAC KIDS

Big Bad Beans

•

Beverly Lewis

BETHANY HOUSE PUBLISHERS
MINNEAPOLIS, MINNESOTA 55438

Published by Bethany House Publishers
11400 Hampshire Avenue South
Bloomington, Minnesota 55438
www.bethanyhouse.com

Bethany House Publishers is a Division of
Baker Book House Company, Grand Rapids, Michigan.

Printed in the United States of America

Library of Congress Cataloging-in-Publication Data
Lewis, Beverly, 1949–
   [Mountain bikes & garbanzo beans]
   Big bad beans / by Beverly Lewis.
      p. cm. — (The cul-de-sac kids ; 22)
   Previously publishes as: Mountain bikes & garbanzo
beans.
   SUMMARY: Although his scheme to get out of eating his
mother's health food nearly ruins his plan to save money for
a bike, Jason finally finds success in an unexpected way.
   ISBN 0–7642–2127–2
[1. Bicycles and bicycling Fiction. 2. Christian life Fiction.]
I. Title. II. Series: Lewis, Beverly, 1949–   Cul-de-sac
kids ; 22.
PZ7.L58464 Bi   2000   99–6753
[Fic]—dc21   CIP

For my son Jonathan,
who agrees with Jason Birchall
about the "big bad beans."

THE CUL-DE-SAC KIDS

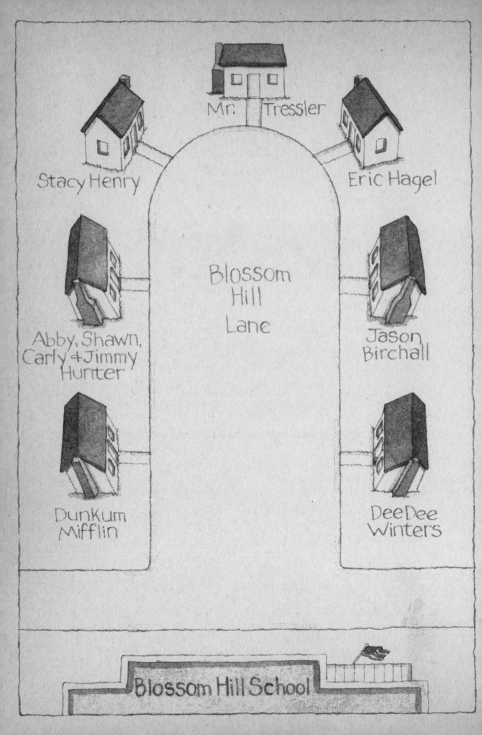

ONE

Jason Birchall pushed through his dresser drawer. He shoved his baseball cards and comic books aside.

His hand bumped the old cardboard box in the corner. His money box! It was a top-secret place where he kept his life savings.

"Jason!" his mother called. "Your after-school snack is ready."

"Super yuck," Jason muttered.

He was tired of his mother's healthy diet. He was even starting to have carrot and celery nightmares. Last night, three giant carrots chased him to school!

Jason emptied his jeans pockets. He placed seven dollar bills in a row on his dresser. Then he counted again.

Doing yard work for Stacy Henry's mom was super cool. Only ten more dollars to go. Soon, Eric Hagel's mountain bike would belong to him.

Ya-hoo! Jason could hardly wait.

He folded the seven dollar bills. Then he stuffed them into his money box.

Hiding the box was a smart thing to do. He pushed it way back, into the corner of the drawer.

Suddenly, he spied a pack of bubble gum. His mouth began to water. He could almost taste the sweet, gooey gum.

How long had it been since he'd chewed bubble gum?

Weeks ago his mother had read a silly health-food book. *"Time for some big changes,"* she'd said.

Maybe the diet was OK for her and

Dad, but Jason wanted sweets. He wadded up four pieces of bubble gum and smashed them into his mouth.

"Jason, dear," Mother called again.

Phooey!

The bubble gum had to go. But Jason didn't want to swallow it. That would be real dumb. He would save the sugary wad for later.

Quickly, he stuck the gum on the wrapper. And—*wham!*—he closed the drawer.

Safe!

"I'm coming." He hurried to his bedroom door.

Mother was standing in the hallway, holding a tray of sliced carrots and celery sticks.

"Double yuck," Jason said. He stared at the orange and green vegetables. He wrinkled up his face at them.

"Aren't you hungry?" Mother said, inching the tray closer.

12

"Not for this stuff," he said.

"Have you been snitching sweets?" Mother asked.

Jason shook his head no. He had stuck to the diet. Anyway, gum didn't count.

His mother smiled. "This snack will do you good."

Jason shrugged. He took a handful of the orange and green health sticks.

When his mother left, he pulled the junk drawer open again. There he found his wad of bubble gum. He sniffed the strawberry flavor.

Yum-m-m! His favorite!

Jason looked at the carrots and celery sticks in his hand. "Better stay out of my dreams tonight," he warned.

Then he took his first bite. He gobbled the raw vegetables down—to get it over with. He couldn't wait to get the horrible taste out of his mouth.

He reached for the wad of bubble gum and stuffed his face. Jason tiptoed to the bedroom door and peeked out. All clear! Mother was nowhere in sight.

Fast as a super-spider, he tiptoed down the hall to the front door. Time to visit Eric Hagel next door. Time to check out the flashy mountain bike.

Soon it'll be mine! thought Jason.

TWO

Jason ran next door to Eric's house. He nearly stumbled over Stacy Henry. She was sitting near the driveway, staring at some black ants.

"Hey, Stacy," he said. "What're you doing?"

"Nothing much." She looked up. "What're *you* doing?"

"I have to talk to Eric," he told her.

"He's busy cleaning out the garage." She pointed toward the house. "In there."

Jason hurried up the driveway and leaned against the side of the garage door.

"Looks like you're working too hard," he teased.

Eric stopped sweeping. "What's up?"

Jason wandered in and looked around. "How clean does your garage have to be?"

"Clean enough to earn my allowance," Eric replied.

"Looks good to me," Jason said.

Eric laughed. "Tell my mom that."

Jason spotted the mountain bike. It was parked in the corner of the garage. "When are you getting your *new* bike?" he asked.

"Next week, if you come up with the money for my old one," Eric explained.

Jason danced around. "I only need ten more bucks," he said.

"That's a lot," Eric said. "Where are you gonna get it?"

Jason shrugged. "Beats me, but I will!"

He turned and watched Stacy. She was letting ants crawl over her fingers on the

sunny cement. "Hey, Stacy," he called. "Does your mom need any more help in her garden?"

"Don't think so," Stacy replied.

"Maybe Abby Hunter can give you some ideas," Eric said. "The president of the Cul-de-sac Kids oughta be able to think of something, right?"

Jason laughed. "Me, work with a girl?"

"You helped my mom," Stacy spoke up. "*She's* a girl."

"That's different," Jason muttered. He eyed Eric's bike and moved toward it.

Just ten more bucks, he thought. He touched the shiny frame. The golden flecks shone through the royal blue. It was easy to imagine himself speeding down Blossom Hill Lane. His old bike was trash. "I have to have this bike," he whispered. "Have to!"

"It's yours when you cough up the money," Eric reminded him.

Jason was startled. Eric had heard him.

"Well, I'll see you later," Jason said.

He crossed the street to Abby's house. Her father was outside shooting baskets. Mr. Hunter tossed the ball to Jason.

"Is Abby home?" Jason asked.

"She's shopping with her mother," Mr. Hunter said.

Jason turned and shot. He made a basket first try.

Across the street, Eric hopped on his old bike. He flew past Abby's house and down the street.

Jason watched him go. "Where's *he* headed?" he whispered.

He aimed the ball and shot. It bounced off the rim.

Just then Mr. Hunter's pager beeped. With a smile, he waved to Jason and rushed inside.

Jason stood holding the basketball. He didn't like the idea of waiting around for

Abby. Why couldn't *he* think of a way to earn the extra money?

★ ★ ★

At supper, Jason poked at the salad on his plate. He played with his lettuce and sprouts. He glared at the garbanzo beans. "Why must we eat these big, bad beans?" he whined.

"They're good for you," his mother said. "That's why."

"But they stick in my throat," he argued.

His father spoke up. "You might try chewing them, son."

Jason tried, but it was no use. The beans tasted horrible. And they were too big to swallow whole, like a pill.

He waited till his parents weren't looking. Then he sneaked some beans to Muffie. His new puppy would eat them. She loved people food. Any kind!

Just then the doorbell rang.

Jason leaped from the table.

There stood Eric at the front door. "I've gotta tell you something," Eric said. Then he flipped the kickstand down on the blue mountain bike.

"What's up?" Jason asked.

Eric scratched his head. He was acting strange. "Someone else wants to buy my bike. He'll give me five more bucks than you."

Jason felt his neck grow warm. "Is that where you zoomed off today? To sell your bike to someone else?"

Eric's wide eyes blinked three times. "Yeah, guess so," he said.

"But . . . we had a deal," Jason urged. His breath was coming fast. "You can't change your mind now!"

Eric stared at Jason. "Well, can you match it?"

"You want more money?" Jason asked.

"Here's the deal." Eric rubbed his fingers together. "Whoever's first with the bucks."

Jason stared at the bike. What a super-cool bike. "I'm already ten dollars short," he muttered.

"Too bad, then." Eric turned to go.

The lump in his throat made Jason cough. "There's just no way," he said.

THREE

Jason marched over to Abby's the next day.

He told her his plan to buy Eric's mountain bike. And he told her about Eric's deal—the rotten one.

Abby shook her head. "Sounds like you need some quick money. I know just the thing—a recycling project."

"A what?" Jason asked.

"You know, a recycling project. Care for the earth and pick up some extra cash at the same time. I'll call the Cul-de-sac Kids to help," she said.

"Ya-hoo!" shouted Jason. "When do we start?"

Abby sat on the porch step. "Tomorrow's Saturday. Meet me in front of my house at eight."

"Gotcha." Jason raced home to count the money in his box. One more time.

★ ★ ★

Saturday morning, Jason met Abby in front of her house.

Dee Dee Winters and Abby's little sister, Carly, pulled wagons. Stacy Henry wore her mother's garden gloves.

Dunkum Mifflin showed up with armloads of trash bags. Abby and Carly's Korean brothers, Shawn and Jimmy, helped carry the bags.

Jason smiled. He felt good having so many friends. Cul-de-sac Kid friends!

Only Eric was missing.

But Jason didn't care. He'd show Eric all about good deals. He'd have the money soon. Maybe even today!

"If you buy Eric's mountain bike, I'll race you," Dee Dee teased.

"We sure will!" Carly piped up.

Jason pushed up his glasses. He had more important things on his mind than bike races. At least for now.

Dunkum whistled with his fingers. "We'll stop at every house in the cul-de-sac. Then all the houses up the street from the school. Abby, Stacy, and I will gather newspapers. Carly and Dee Dee can pull the glass bottles in the wagons. Jason, you, Shawn, and Jimmy can collect aluminum cans." Dunkum gave Jason a handful of heavy-duty trash bags. "We'll split the money evenly," he said.

"Super good," Jason said.

Abby grinned. "Let's go to Eric's house first," she suggested.

"Hoo-ray!" the kids agreed.

"This is a fun way to earn money," Dee Dee said.

Carly hurried to catch up with Dee Dee.

Shawn and Jimmy Hunter chattered in Korean.

Abby, Stacy, and Dunkum told jokes.

Jason jigged and jived.

By lunchtime, the kids had gathered a mountain of recyclable items. Enough to fill Abby's father's van.

Jason, Abby, and Dunkum rode along to the recycling center.

On the way back, Jason counted his share of the money. Fifteen dollars and forty-eight cents worth of work.

Yes! He ran across the street to Eric's. No one was home.

Phooey, he thought.

Eager to buy the bike, Jason darted home. He went to his room and counted *all* his money. For the last time.

Jason wanted to dance. There was plenty of money to buy Eric's bike!

★ ★ ★

At lunch, he ate fish and salad without fussing. But he nearly choked on the garbanzo beans. He excused himself every few minutes to see if Eric was home yet.

His mom went to the kitchen for more herbal tea.

His dad reached for the TV remote and turned on The Weather Channel.

Quickly, Jason offered his last garbanzo bean to Muffie. The puppy chomped it right down.

Ya-hoo!

Jason didn't bother to excuse himself from the table. He hurried off to his room.

There he rooted through his junk drawer. *Gotta have some strawberry bubble gum,* he thought. *Gotta, gotta!*

Just then he heard Eric's grandpa drive up.

"Yes!" He grabbed his money and slammed the drawer. The bubble gum would just have to wait. Again.

Eric's grandpa was pulling into the garage when Jason arrived. Jason waited for Eric and his grandpa to get out of the car.

"I've got the money," Jason shouted, waving it in Eric's face. "Even the extra five bucks!"

Eric made a smirky face. "Too late," he said. "The bike's not for sale."

Jason stared at Eric in the dimly lit garage. He was too stunned to speak.

Eric dug his hand into his pocket. He waved a bunch of dollar bills. "Sorry, someone beat you to it," he said.

"No way!" Jason shouted. "That's not fair!"

"A deal's a deal," Eric said. Then he turned and trudged into the house.

Jason wanted to holler and carry on.

But it was no use.

FOUR

Jason slipped in through the back door. He tiptoed down the hall to his room. The floor squeaked on the way.

"Jason, is that you?" his mother called from the living room.

Rats! She'd want him to eat another healthy snack.

What *he* wanted was to chew up three packs of bubble gum. He wished he had two hundred packs of gum. The healthy diet bugged him.

"Jason?" came his mother's voice again.

He looked at the clock. "Time for the carrot and celery brigade," he whispered.

Sure enough. Here came his mother with a full tray.

Jason picked out two skinny celery sticks and three short carrot sticks. He waited till his mother left the room. Then he lifted his mattress and stuffed the orange and green sticks underneath.

"That's where veggie sticks belong," he muttered.

Then he headed for his junk drawer. He could almost taste his yummy strawberry bubble gum!

★ ★ ★

The next morning, Jason watched Abby Hunter's family climb into their van. Every Sunday they attended church. Always together.

Stacy Henry, Abby's best friend, was going along. So was Dunkum Mifflin, the best hoop shooter around. And little Dee

Dee Winters. Seven Cul-de-sac Kids, counting the Hunter kids.

They could almost have a club meeting, thought Jason with a sigh.

Abby often asked Jason to go with them. Dunkum did, too.

But Jason gave her plenty of excuses. For one thing, he wasn't used to going to church. For another, his dress-up clothes were too small.

"None of that matters," Abby always said.

But Jason refused to go.

After the van left, he wandered outside. He sat on the front step and stared at Eric's house. *The lousy double-crosser better stay inside all day,* he thought.

Hey! Now, Eric—*there* was a kid for Sunday school and church!

★ ★ ★

The Hunters' van arrived back around noon.

31

Jason was still sitting on the step. Bored silly.

Abby ran across the street. "Hi, Jason."

"What's up?" he asked.

"Plenty," she said, out of breath. "Can you hide something for me?"

Jason pushed up his glasses. "Maybe."

Abby opened her purse. She pulled out a sandwich bag full of dollar bills.

"Wow," said Jason. "That's a bunch of money."

"Shh! It's for Mother's Day," Abby whispered. "And it's top secret."

"Really?"

She handed the plastic money bag to him. "I can't seem to hide this anymore. I think someone's found my hiding place."

"Like who?"

"I'm not sure," Abby replied.

Jason clutched her bag of bills. "Your bucks are safe with me!"

"Double dabble good!" She turned to

cross the street. "Thanks, Jason."

"How long should I hide the you-know-what?" Jason called to her.

"I'll need it next Saturday. Dad and I are going shopping for Mother's Day," Abby said. "But don't tell anyone. OK?"

Jason nodded. "It's a double-done deal."

Abby smiled. "Thanks again." She turned to go but stopped in the middle of the street. "How's the bike deal coming?" she asked.

Suddenly, Jason felt sick. "Oh, that," he said.

Abby frowned hard. "What's wrong?"

Jason sat stone still. Should he tell on Eric?

"C'mon, Jason. Did you buy the bike or not?" she asked.

"Eric double-crossed me," he blurted.

Abby's eyes nearly popped out. "You're kidding . . . how?"

"He sold the bike out from under my nose," Jason said.

He felt horrible as soon as he said it. Worse than ever!

FIVE

Jason wished Abby would stop staring at him. He could see she wasn't leaving. Not until he explained.

"Eric sold his bike to someone else," he repeated. "That's all there is to it."

Abby sighed. "This is double dabble rotten."

"It's not your fault," he said.

Abby sat beside him on the step. "I can't believe this."

"He's a double-crosser, that's what," Jason said.

Abby nodded her head. "No kidding."

Dunkum came up the street just then. He was dribbling his basketball. "Wanna play?" he asked Jason.

"Not today," Jason replied.

Dunkum stopped bouncing the ball. He looked first at Jason, then at Abby. "Who died?" he asked.

Abby's face drooped. "Nobody," she said.

"Could've fooled me," Dunkum said. He twirled the basketball on his finger. "Come on, Jason, let's shoot some hoops."

"Don't feel like it," Jason replied.

Dunkum raised his eyebrows. "Why not?"

Abby stood up. "I better get going," she said.

"See ya," Jason called.

Dunkum and Jason headed for the far end of the street. It was the dead end of the cul-de-sac. A grassy place with a large oak tree, near Mr. Tressler's house.

Dunkum leaned against the old tree.

He tossed his basketball to the ground. "What's going on?" he asked.

"Don't ask," Jason said.

Dunkum frowned and let the subject drop. He pulled a black book from his back pocket. "Check this out," he said.

Jason sat on the ground, eyeing the tiny book. "What is it?"

"It's a New Testament. I got it the first time I went to Abby's church." He paused for a second. "I've learned lots of verses from it."

"What's so great about that?" Jason asked.

Dunkum grinned. "If I say all the verses by next Sunday, I'll win another ribbon. Then I'll have twenty-five. Maybe I'll even win the grand prize!"

Jason didn't give a hoot about church prizes. He was thinking about the bike that got away.

"Here," Dunkum said. He handed the pocket Bible to Jason. "Follow along and

see if I've got my verses right. OK?"

"Whatever," Jason complained. "If you *have* to."

So Dunkum began.

Halfway through the first verse, Jason stopped him. "Wrong. You're mixed up," he said.

Dunkum started over. But he missed more words.

"You were real close." Jason closed the book. "I oughta go home now. Mom's leafy lunch is calling."

Dunkum nodded. "Thanks. Can you help me again?" he asked.

"Maybe," Jason said, getting up. He wiped his hands on his jeans.

They hurried down Blossom Hill Lane. Jason pushed his hand deep into his pants pocket. Yes! Abby's money was safe there.

"Wanna come to church next Sunday?" asked Dunkum. "It's Mother's Day. Bring your mom and get a rose."

Jason scratched his head. "She'd like that."

They walked past Eric's house. Jason looked the other way on purpose.

"See ya later," Dunkum said. He darted across the street. The basketball danced under one leg. "Come over Wednesday after school," he called. "I'll have my verses ready by then."

"I guess so," said Jason. He didn't see what was so special about saying Bible verses from memory. Except maybe for the grand prize. Whatever *that* was.

After lunch, he went to his room and opened his junk drawer. Abby's cash fit into his cardboard money box. He stacked up a pile of baseball cards between her money and his. Abby's Mother's Day money was on the left and his money was on the right.

Super good!

Now . . . he needed to find another used bike to buy. Everything would be

hoo-ray good, if he could.

Quickly, Jason emptied his other pocket. Big, bad garbanzo beans were inside. He'd sneaked them off his plate at lunch.

Surely Mom could come up with something better than yucky bean salads. But if not, he'd have to hide them in his junk drawer. They'd be fine there until trash day.

Wednesday!

SIX

It was Monday.

Jason's class lined up for art. They were making pop-up heart vases from construction paper. For Mother's Day.

Eric put glue bottles on each table. When he passed Jason's table, he bragged about his new mountain bike. "I'm getting it in two days," he said.

Jason felt sick again. All the Cul-de-sac Kids had cool bikes. Even Dee Dee Winters.

Abby sat across from him at the table. She was helping the new girl follow the pattern, fold, and cut the pages.

Jason watched her do what she did best—help others. He wanted to thank her for helping him raise money for Eric's bike. Eric's dumb old mountain bike. The one he never bought!

The word was out by morning recess. Eric had double-crossed Jason. Everyone knew about it. Even the little kids!

Bossy Dee Dee warned Jason about eating chocolate bars with his leftover bike money. "You'll spoil your mother's plans for your health," she teased.

"Mind your own business." He turned away to find a soccer game.

"It's not the only bike in the world," Dee Dee said.

Maybe to her it wasn't. But Dee Dee hadn't felt the smooth, shiny frame, its golden flecks smiling through the blue. She hadn't heard the whir of its jazzy tire spokes.

Br-ring! The bell rang.

Everyone raced to the school. Everyone except Jason. He dragged his feet.

★ ★ ★

After school on Wednesday, Jason went straight home.

He tossed pieces of lettuce and three wrinkled garbanzo beans from his lunch into the junk drawer. His money and Abby's money was safely hidden in the corner.

Then he headed to Dunkum's house. Time to help him practice Bible verses.

Dunkum stood tall beside his desk.

Jason sat on the bed, checking the words in the New Testament.

"Galations 6:2: 'Carry each other's burdens, and in this way you will fulfill the law of Christ.' "

"You said it perfectly!" said Jason. "Now what?"

"Luke 3:11: 'The man with two tunics should share with him who has none, and

the one who has food should do the same.' "

"That's correct." Jason handed the New Testament back. "Wow, I didn't know the Bible said stuff like that."

"Me either," said Dunkum. "Not till I found out at Abby's church." He headed for the garage.

Jason followed. "So are you gonna do it?"

"Do what?" Dunkum reached for his basketball.

"You know, share some *real* food with me. Like it says in the Bible," Jason said.

"Oh, no, you don't." Dunkum shot two baskets. "I won't be responsible for messing with your mom's diet."

"But it's a real yucky diet. Garbanzo beans and lettuce—junk like that. Nobody knows how horrible it is." Jason sat on an old bench in the corner. He watched Dunkum do his fancy footwork.

Zing! The ball went right in. Perfect shot.

"Your turn," Dunkum said.

"Are you gonna win the grand prize at church on Sunday?" Jason asked.

"Hope so," Dunkum answered. He whirled around and swished the ball through the hoop.

"What's the prize?" Jason asked.

"Hot new Rollerblades," Dunkum said, out of breath.

"Really?" He bounced the ball and took a shot. In!

"That's what I'm trying for," Dunkum said. "I'm tired of riding my bikes anyway. Playing ball is *my* thing. But blading . . . I could practice basketball on them."

Jason stopped bouncing the ball. "Did you say *bikes*? You got more than one?"

"Sure. You remember my old road bike. Plus, my dad bought me a brand-new BMX. I hardly ever ride them anymore," Dunkum said.

47

"How come?" Jason couldn't believe his ears.

"Basketball is my life." Dunkum fired one up. The ball swished right through. Nothing but net!

At that moment, Jason had a new idea. He took a deep breath. "Wanna sell one of your bikes?"

Dunkum stopped. He wiped his face on his sleeve. "Hey, good idea. The road bike needs some paint. That's all."

"Ya-hoo!" shouted Jason. "How much?"

"Whatever you got," Dunkum said. He dribbled the ball behind his back.

"Don't go away!" Jason hurried home to get the money. He could trust Dunkum any day. He was not a double-crosser.

SEVEN

Jason flew to his room.

The place was a mess. Pajamas and towels were crumpled in a heap in the corner. The bed was lumpy. His dresser drawers yawned open, and jeans played peekaboo over the top.

He kicked away pieces of gum wrapper with his foot.

Gum wrappers?

What were *they* doing out?

He scrambled to his knees and pushed the comic books aside. The junk drawer was junkier than ever!

Searching, he found his bike money in the back of the drawer. The baseball cards divided his money on the right from Abby's on the . . .

"Wha-at's this?" he wailed.

Abby's money was all ripped up! Bits of garbanzo beans were mixed in with shredded dollar bills.

"What happened?" Jason cried. "Who did this?"

A trail of the scrappy mess led to the bathroom. He found his puppy whining in the corner of the shower.

"Bad, bad Muffie!" He wanted to shake her. No, that was too kind. He wanted to hang Muffie up by her doggie ears.

"How could you do this?" he shouted.

Muffie yipped and backed into the shower stall.

Jason slammed the bathroom door and looked in the mirror. He yelled at his own face. "Can't you do anything right?"

He slapped himself on the forehead.

"It was those big, bad beans!" Jason exclaimed. "I should've known . . . I should've . . ."

His mother knocked on the door. "Jason, are you all right?"

"I'm doomed. Abby's money is all gone! Muffie ate it!" he said over and over.

"I can't understand you," his mother said.

"Everything's wrong," he muttered. "Abby counted on me and now . . ."

He picked Muffie out of the shower. Her breath smelled like beans. "You little sneak," he hollered in the pooch's face. "I oughta call the dog pound this minute!"

Poor little Muffie shook in his arms. He carried her to the back door and put her out. Then he slammed the kitchen door and headed for his room.

The junk drawer was sagging open. Half a garbanzo bean and some lettuce were scattered in the front—the reason for Muffie's mischief.

But deep inside, Jason knew it was his own fault.

He groaned. *Those good-for-nothing beans! If only I'd cleaned my plate.*

Just then the doorbell rang.

"Jason," called his mother. "Your friend Abby's here to see you."

His heart sank. Abby had come for her Mother's Day money early. He was almost positive!

Jason breathed fast and hard. How much money had she given him? How many dollar bills?

On the floor behind the door he spied the sandwich baggie. The amount was written on a round pink sticker.

Twenty-two dollars!

Jason gasped. What could he do?

Quickly, he counted his own money. It was all there.

He thought about Dunkum's terrific road bike down the street. Just waiting to be his!

But he had no choice. Jason stuffed his own money into the sandwich bag. He would give it all to Abby Hunter. She'd never know what happened to her half-eaten money. Or worse—that he couldn't be counted on.

He shuffled down the hall. No bike for a kid with a health-food freak for a dog!

"I'm coming, Abby," he called.

Jason tried to swallow the lump in his throat. It was very hard.

EIGHT

Br-ring! The phone rang right after Abby left.

Jason ran to get it. "Hello," he said.

"Where *are* you?" Dunkum asked. "I thought you were coming back to buy my road bike."

"I was, but . . ." Jason stopped. "Mom is real sick and she needs me here." It was a lie.

"Sorry about that," Dunkum said. "Tomorrow after school, then?"

"Uh . . . no. I can't come then, either." Jason quickly made up another story.

"Abby and I are working on a science project."

"What project?" Dunkum asked.

"I . . . I . . . uh, have to go," Jason said.

He stared at the phone and felt lousy. He'd lied to Dunkum. Two times!

★ ★ ★

The next day, Jason avoided Dunkum at morning recess.

But Dunkum cornered him in the afternoon. "You're acting weird," Dunkum said. "How come?"

Jason's face felt hot. His hands were sweaty. "I guess I don't tell lies very well," he confessed.

"You lied to me?" Dunkum looked puzzled. "About what?"

Jason stumbled over his words. "I lied . . . about . . . about why I didn't buy your bike."

"You did?"

He didn't want to tell Dunkum about

Muffie eating Abby's money. He didn't want Abby to find out. She would think he couldn't be counted on. That would be horrible!

"It's a long story," Jason said. "You'd never believe it anyway."

"That's OK," said Dunkum. "You don't have to buy my bike if you don't want to. I just thought . . ."

"But I *do* wanna buy it. More than anything," Jason said.

"So . . . what's the problem?" Dunkum asked.

Jason thought about it. Should he spill the beans?

"I'll tell you if you keep it quiet," he said at last.

Dunkum nodded. "I won't tell. Scout's honor."

"No fooling?" Jason begged for a promise.

"No fooling," Dunkum said.

Jason told the truth this time. Every bit of it.

Dunkum stared at him. "You're kidding. You used your own money so Abby wouldn't know hers got eaten by Muffie?"

Jason pulled out his pocket linings. "See? I'm broke," he said. "Busted."

"Let me get this straight," Dunkum said. "You gave Abby the money you made from our recycling project? The bucks that were gonna buy you some cool wheels?"

"It wasn't easy, but that's the truth. The *real* story," Jason said.

"Wow! That is some act of charity," Dunkum said.

"Huh?" Jason pushed up his glasses.

"Charity. You know . . . kindness. When you give because you care." Dunkum pushed his hair back.

Jason laughed. "Sounds like a Mother's Day card."

"Hey, no kidding. We talked about that

in Sunday school last week," Dunkum said.

"Really? You talk about stuff like that?" Jason asked.

"Sure. Have you ever heard this before: 'It is better to give than to receive'?" Dunkum was grinning.

Jason snapped his fingers. "Some wise old saying, right?"

Dunkum nodded. "Better than wise. It's in the Bible."

"Mixed in with those verses about sharing food?" Jason asked.

Dunkum laughed out loud.

"Gotcha," teased Jason.

Dunkum's smile faded. "See you at church this Sunday?" he asked.

"If I come, will you say your verses? About sharing and feeding kids on dumb diets?" added Jason. "I wouldn't wanna miss that."

"You bet!" Dunkum seemed pleased. "Bring your mother and get a rose."

The school bell rang.

Jason and Dunkum hurried inside.

Jason felt super great. He wondered how he could pass a feeling like this on to Eric, the double-crosser. The new mountain-bike owner, the rotten . . .

No, he wouldn't even think that. He'd keep his thoughts to himself.

Miss Hershey stood up. She gave the math assignment. "Class, please turn to page 118," she said. "Begin by solving problem number one. And be sure to show your work."

Jason could hardly believe his eyes. The math problem was about four boys in a marathon bike race.

A mountain-bike race!

NINE

What a sunny Mother's Day!

Jason and his mom attended Abby's church. The pastor gave them each a small New Testament. Just like Dunkum's.

Jason crossed his fingers when Dunkum said his verses. After Dunkum was finished, Jason said, "You did it! Go, Dunkum!"

Abby clapped her hands. "Dunkum's double dabble good!"

Jason thought Abby was pretty cool, too. For a girl, of course.

"Now for the grand prize," Abby whispered. She took her place beside Dunkum and three others.

Dunkum was up against four girls!

Jason listened to each verse. And he decided something right then. The Bible verses were much better than just wise old sayings. He looked down at his New Testament. Carefully, he held it with both hands.

Soon the first round was finished.

Whew, that was close! thought Jason. He really hoped Dunkum would win.

Next, it was Abby's turn. She was super at saying her verses. *She oughta be*, he thought. Abby had been doing this all her life.

Things were much different for Dunkum. He was new at this.

At last, the final round came.

The girls wrinkled their noses or twisted their hair before reciting each verse.

62

One girl forgot the chapter and verse but said the book of the Bible. She was out.

Her mistake was catching. The other girls forgot a word, too.

Dunkum looked very relaxed. Was he thinking about basketball or the grand prize? Or both?

Squeezing his New Testament, Jason rooted for Dunkum. He felt like cheering or dancing. But he sat quietly, hard as it was.

"Dunkum Mifflin," the teacher said. "Please say Luke 3:11."

Dunkum paused. He glanced at the ceiling.

Jason watched and waited. *C'mon, you can do it*, he thought.

Even Jason remembered this verse. It was a real good one! About sharing junk food with a kid on a health diet.

The teacher looked at her stopwatch. "Five seconds to go."

Jason's heart leaped up.

The air was tense. The suspense was too much.

Just as the teacher started to raise her hand, Dunkum began, " 'The man with two tunics should share them with him who has none, and the one who has food should do the same.' Luke 3:11," he said.

Jason sighed.

Abby was next. It looked like she was holding her breath. Jason couldn't tell for sure.

The teacher said another verse. Abby had to tell where it was found. The backward approach.

Very tricky, thought Jason.

There was a long silence.

Abby turned to Dunkum. "I don't think I know that one," she admitted.

"You have five seconds," the teacher said again.

Abby looked up. She looked down. She shook her folded hands.

"Time's up" came the teacher's voice.

Dunkum was the grand-prize winner! Everyone clapped for both Dunkum and Abby.

Abby was the second-place winner. Her eyes danced as she shook Dunkum's hand.

What a good sport! thought Jason. He shot her a thumbs-up.

"Thanks, Jason," Abby said as she sat down.

Dunkum took a seat beside him. "Abby's a winner at losing," Dunkum whispered. "Get it?"

"She sure is. Now what?" Jason asked.

"The grand prize!" said Dunkum.

Jason stood up and did a quicky jig. He just had to!

TEN

After church, Jason opened the car door for Dunkum. He helped load Dunkum's grand prize into the van.

On the ride home, they checked out the slick new Rollerblades.

Abby and her little sister, Carly, leaned over the seat for a closer look. Her brothers, Shawn and Jimmy, looked, too.

"Wow! Your Rollerblades are double dabble terrific!" said Abby.

"How many verses total?" Abby's father asked Dunkum.

Dunkum grinned. "Twenty-five," he said.

"Amazing," said Jason's mom. She was holding two Mother's Day roses.

Jason's stomach was beginning to growl. He excused the rumble. "Sorry . . . I'm just hungry," he said.

His mother's face beamed. "There's a surprise in the oven."

"Real food, I hope?" asked Jason.

"How does meatloaf sound for a change?" said his mother.

"Ya-hoo!"

Dunkum stuffed his fancy Roller-blades back in the box. "I've been thinking, Jason. What if I just *give* you my road bike?"

Jason couldn't believe his ears. "You'd do that?" he said.

"Sure . . . why not?" Dunkum pushed the lid down. "I've got what I want right here." He tapped on the box. "And in here." He patted his chest.

"You've gotta be kidding," Jason said.

"The verses aren't just in my head anymore. They're in my heart, too," Dunkum explained.

Jason held his New Testament real tight. He was beginning to understand what Dunkum meant.

Dunkum tapped his fingers on the grand-prize box. "Luke 3:11—*my* way—says: If you have two bikes, which I do, share with Jason, who doesn't have even one."

Abby was laughing. "Dunkum would make a good preacher," she said.

Blossom Hill Lane came into view. The van turned the corner to the cul-de-sac.

Jason jittered, eager to get out. "This was some cool Mother's Day," he said.

His mother smiled. "Thank you for inviting us," she told Abby's parents.

"You're welcome anytime." Abby had a sparkle in her eye.

"How about next Sunday?" asked Jason.

"Hoo-ray!" cheered Dunkum, climbing out of the van. "Hey, come over after dinner and pick up your new bike."

Jason's mother smiled. "Better check with your parents first," she said.

"I will," Dunkum said and hurried home.

Jason crossed the street with his mother. "Happy Mother's Day, Mom," he said.

"Thanks, Jason." She smelled the roses, then handed him one. "Is there a reason why we got *two* roses?" she asked. There was a twinkle in her eye.

Jason held the front door open. He smelled the oven dinner waiting inside. "No big, bad beans today?" he asked.

His mother smiled. "It's time for another change."

"Yes!" Jason shouted and headed for Eric's house.

★ ★ ★

Next door, the house was noisy. Eric's grandpa was mowing the lawn.

Eric was in the garage, shining the spokes on his new bike.

Jason felt uneasy. He held out a long-stemmed rose. "Hi, Eric," he said.

"What's the rose for?" Eric asked.

"Give it to your mom for Mother's Day," Jason said.

"Hey, thanks." Eric looked surprised. Really surprised. "Where'd it come from?"

"Abby's church gave roses to all the mothers," he said.

"That's cool," Eric said.

Jason was dying to ask Eric something. Finally he did. "How do you like your new bike?"

Eric shrugged his shoulders. "It's OK, but I miss my old one."

"You do?"

"I wish I'd kept it. Or sold it to *you*,"

Eric said. "It's already a piece of junk. You would have taken better care of it."

Jason didn't know what to say. Before today he might've felt secretly glad. Glad that Eric messed up by selling his bike to someone else.

Not today. Things were different.

"Well, I gotta go," Jason said.

"What's your hurry?" Eric asked, getting up.

"Got a lunch date with my mother," Jason told him.

"For Mother's Day?" asked Eric. He held the rose stem carefully between two thorns.

"Yep. She makes a mean meatloaf," he said.

"Sounds like total yuck," Eric muttered.

Jason didn't mind. Meatloaf sure did beat out garbanzo beans any day.

And bikes? Dunkum owned two of

them. And thanks to Luke 3:11, one would be his.

Ya-hoo!

THE CUL-DE-SAC KIDS SERIES
Don't Miss #23!
THE UPSIDE-DOWN DAY

It's school spirit day at Blossom Hill School, and everyone's enjoying the fun. Especially Abby Hunter's teacher, Miss Hershey. She wears her clothes backward and does other wacky things.

And there's a new girl at school with a BIG secret. Bethanne DeWitt—with bright red pigtails—dares Abby's class to guess her secret. In just one school day!

Can the Cul-de-sac Kids do it? Or will spunky Bethanne outsmart all of them? Who does this new kid think she is, anyway?

About the Author

Beverly Lewis loved two dogs while growing up in Pennsylvania. One was a white Eskimo spitz named Maxie. The other was a tiny brown cocker spaniel named Trixie. Later, Beverly and her husband and their three children made a home for a white cockapoo called Cuddles. And they loved him for seven happy years.

Maxie, Trixie, and Cuddles were never caught eating garbanzo beans or chewing up dollar bills. So . . . where did the idea for this story come from? "My husband went on a health-food diet for one month," says Beverly. "He made LOTS of salads with garbanzo beans in them." Jonathan, their son, sneaked his big, bad beans (garbanzo beans) to Cuddles. And the dog quickly spit them out!

Each Cul-de-sac Kids book features pets that belong to the kids on Blossom Hill Lane. Which is a real place in Lancaster County, Pennsylvania.

Be sure to collect all the books. You never know what you might be missing!

Also by Beverly Lewis

The Beverly Lewis Amish Heritage Cookbook

GIRLS ONLY (GO!)
Youth Fiction

Dreams on Ice	*Follow the Dream*
Only the Best	*Better Than Best*
A Perfect Match	*Photo Perfect*
Reach for the Stars	*Star Status*

SUMMERHILL SECRETS
Youth Fiction

Whispers Down the Lane	*House of Secrets*
Secret in the Willows	*Echoes in the Wind*
Catch a Falling Star	*Hide Behind the Moon*
Night of the Fireflies	*Windows on the Hill*
A Cry in the Dark	*Shadows Beyond the Gate*

HOLLY'S HEART
Youth Fiction

Best Friend, Worst Enemy	*Straight-A Teacher*
Secret Summer Dreams	*No Guys Pact*
Sealed With a Kiss	*Little White Lies*
The Trouble With Weddings	*Freshman Frenzy*
California Crazy	*Mystery Letters*
Second-Best Friend	*Eight Is Enough*
Good-Bye, Dressel Hills	*It's a Girl Thing*

ABRAM'S DAUGHTERS
Adult Fiction

The Covenant	*The Sacrifice*
The Betrayal	*The Prodigal*

THE HERITAGE OF LANCASTER COUNTY
Adult Fiction

The Shunning	*The Confession*
The Reckoning	

OTHER ADULT FICTION

The Postcard • *The Crossroad*
The Redemption of Sarah Cain
October Song
Sanctuary* • *The Sunroom*

www.BeverlyLewis.com

*with David Lewis

From Bethany House Publishers

Series for Beginning Readers[*]

YOUNG COUSINS MYSTERIES
by Elspeth Campbell Murphy

Rib-tickling mysteries just for beginning readers—with Timothy, Titus, and Sarah-Jane from the THREE COUSINS DETECTIVE CLUB®.

WATCH OUT FOR JOEL!
by Sigmund Brouwer

Seven-year-old Joel is always getting into scrapes—despite his older brother, Ricky, always being told, "Watch out for Joel!"

Series for Young Readers†

ASTROKIDS™
by Robert Elmer

Space scooters? Floating robots? Jupiter ice cream? Blast into the future for out-of-this-world, zero-gravity fun with the AstroKids on space station *CLEO-7*.

THE CUL-DE-SAC KIDS
by Beverly Lewis

Each story in this lighthearted series features the hilarious antics and predicaments of nine endearing boys and girls who live on Blossom Hill Lane.

JANETTE OKE'S ANIMAL FRIENDS
by Janette Oke

Endearing creatures from the farm, forest, and zoo discover their place in God's world through various struggles, mishaps, and adventures.

THREE COUSINS DETECTIVE CLUB®
by Elspeth Campbell Murphy

Famous detective cousins Timothy, Titus, and Sarah-Jane learn compelling Scripture-based truths while finding—and solving—intriguing mysteries.

[*](ages 6–8)   †(ages 7–10)